For Jackson Lee

American edition published in 2011 by Andersen Press USA, an imprint of Andersen Press Ltd.
www.andersenpressusa.com

First published in Great Britain in 2011 by Andersen Press Ltd.,
20 Vauxhall Bridge Road, London SW1V 2SA.
Published in Australia by Random House Australia Pty.,
Level 3, 100 Pacific Highway, North Sydney, NSW 2060.



Distributed in the United States and Canada by
Lerner Publishing Group, Inc.
241 First Avenue North
Minneapolis, MN 55401 U.S.A.
www.lernerbooks.com

Color separated in Switzerland by Photolitho AG, Zürich.
Printed and bound in Singapore by Tien Wah Press.
Tony Ross has used watercolor in this book.

Library of Congress Cataloging-in-Publication Data Available.
ISBN: 978-0-7613-8089-4
This book has been printed on acid-free paper.

A Little Princess Story

# I Want a Party!

E

## Tony Ross

Andersen Press USA

The Little Princess was bored, bored, bored.
"I WANT A PARTY!" she said.

"But it isn't Christmas!" said her mother.
"I don't want a CHRISTMAS party," said the Little Princess.
"I just want a party."

"But it isn't your birthday!" said the King.
"I don't want a BIRTHDAY party," said the Little Princess.
"I just want a party."

So the Little Princess spent the rest of the week writing lots of invitations to her party.

The Cook helped her make a party cake and
the wobbliest Jell-O in the world.

"Can I help?" asked the Prime Minister.
"Yes, please," said the Little Princess.
"You can help me make some party hats."

The General showed the Little Princess
how to play his favorite game.
"No peeking," he said. He knew she liked to cheat.

Every night, the Little Princess dreamed about her party. It was going to be the best party ever.

When the day of the party finally arrived, the Little Princess put on her favorite dress and her best crown.

The King helped her blow up the balloons . . .

the Queen put the finishing touches on the decorations . . .

and the Maid filled the party bags with lots of goodies.

At last, everything was ready for the great party . . .

. . . but nobody came. Nobody at all.

A tear rolled down the Little Princess's cheek.
"Nobody knows about my party!" she sobbed.

Just then, someone knocked on the door.
The Little Princess rushed to open it.
There was only one person there. It was her best friend.

"Hello," said her best friend. "I am having a party next week, and I would like you to come. PLEASE come."
She held out an invitation to the Little Princess.

"Thank you, I would LOVE to come," said the Little Princess.
"Do come in. I have arranged a party, JUST FOR YOU!"

So the Little Princess and her best friend had a wonderful party.
If there is only one guest, it is good if it is your best friend.

And when the party ended, her best
friend left with LOTS of party bags.

"That was the best party EVER!"
said the Little Princess . . .

". . . UNTIL, OF COURSE, NEXT WEEK!"

# Other Little Princess Picture Books

I Want My Light On!

I Want to Do It Myself!

I Want Two Birthdays!

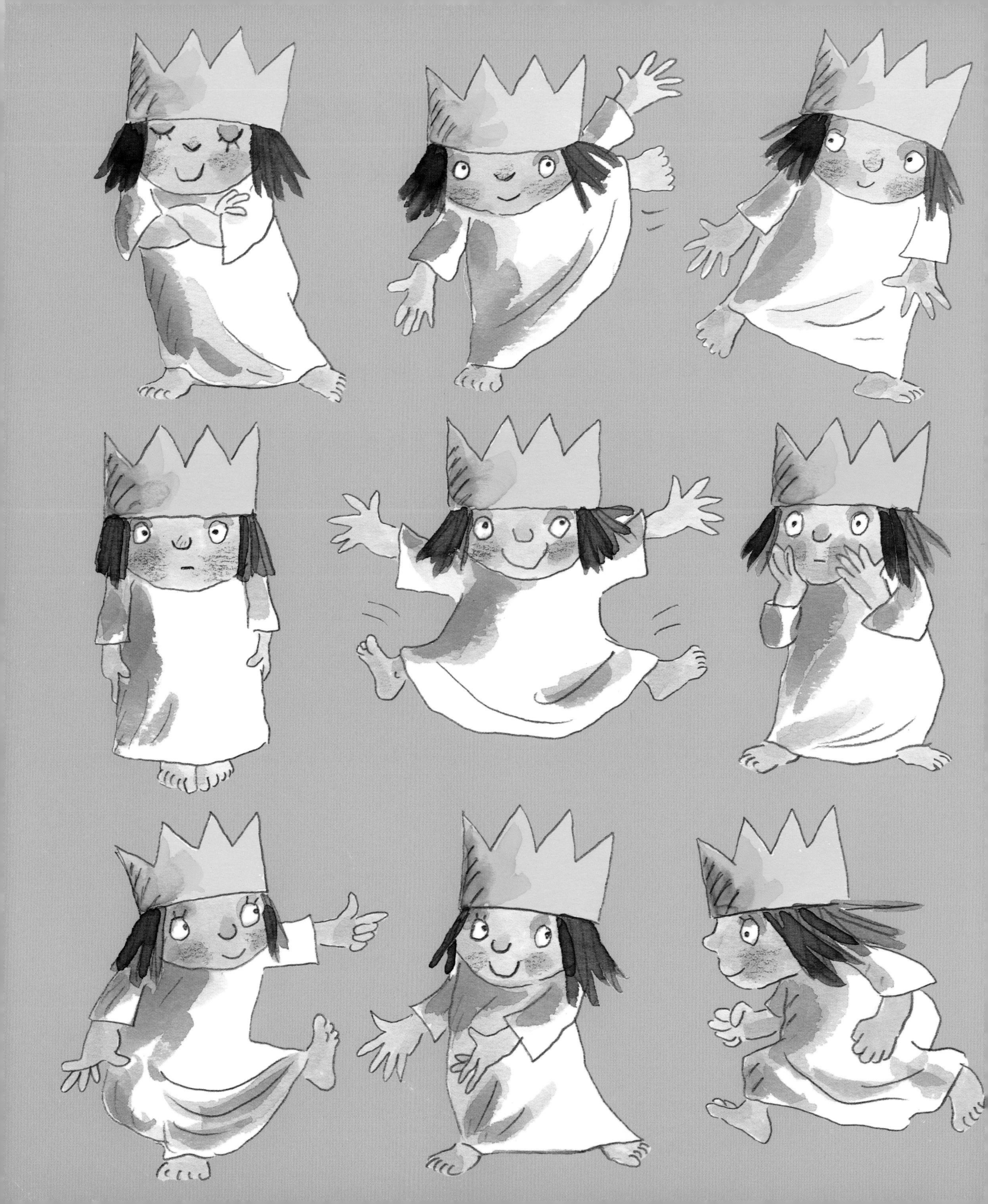